Priscilla

SUPERSTAR!

by Nathaniel Hobbie illustrated by Jocelyn Hobbie

LITTLE, BROWN AND COMPANY

New York ❧ Boston

For Sonja, Vivienne, Lyla, Josie, Isabella, Sofia Hazel and Julian!

Also by Jocelyn Hobbie and Nathaniel Hobbie:

Priscilla and the Pink Planet

Priscilla and the Splish-Splash Surprise

Text copyright © 2007 by Nathaniel Hobbie
Illustrations copyright © 2007 by Jocelyn Hobbie

First Edition: February 2007

Little, Brown and Company

1271 Avenue of the Americas, New York, NY 10020
Visit our Web site at www.lb-kids.com

Library of Congress Cataloging-in-Publication Data

Hobbie, Nathaniel.
 Priscilla superstar! / by Nathaniel Hobbie ; illustrated by Jocelyn Hobbie.—1st ed.
  p. cm.
 Summary: When Priscilla does not get the lead part in the rollerskating school's play she is
disappointed, but instead she gets the part that is just right for her.
 ISBN 0-316-01386-2 (hardcover : alk. paper)
 [1. Roller skating—Fiction. 2. Theater—Fiction. 3. Stories in rhyme.] I. Hobbie, Jocelyn, ill.
II. Title.
PZ8.3.H655Pru 2007
[E]—dc22   2005015394

TWP

Printed in Singapore

Priscilla was looking for something to do.
Something exciting and different and new.

She could go bird-watching or sing in a choir.
Learn to float in mid-air or walk across fire.

Try boating, ballooning. Save habitats.
I just have to sign up. Simple as that!

Well, the Trampoline Troupe made her head spin.

And sewing was torture—that prickly old pin!

In Cooking Creations her soufflé went flat.

Knockball looked fun, but she was shy up at bat.

The Debating Team was too tightly wound.
   The Motorbike Club didn't want her around.
At water ballet there was hair in the pool.
   In Mello-Out meditation she started to drool.

Then came a call from her best friend, Bettina.
"It's opening night for Princess Rollerina!
The show starts at six at Superstar Hall."

"Let's go!" clapped Priscilla. "That sounds like a ball."

Priscilla was perched on the edge of her seat,
wringing her hands and tapping her feet.
The curtains went up and all the lights faded.
The hall became silent. Everyone waited.

There, in the spotlight, Rollerina appeared.
She swept 'cross the stage. The audience cheered.

One moment she spun like a whirling typhoon.

The next she was drifting like clouds past the moon.

She was elegance, grace, power, and speed.
Priscilla got so excited, she practically peed!

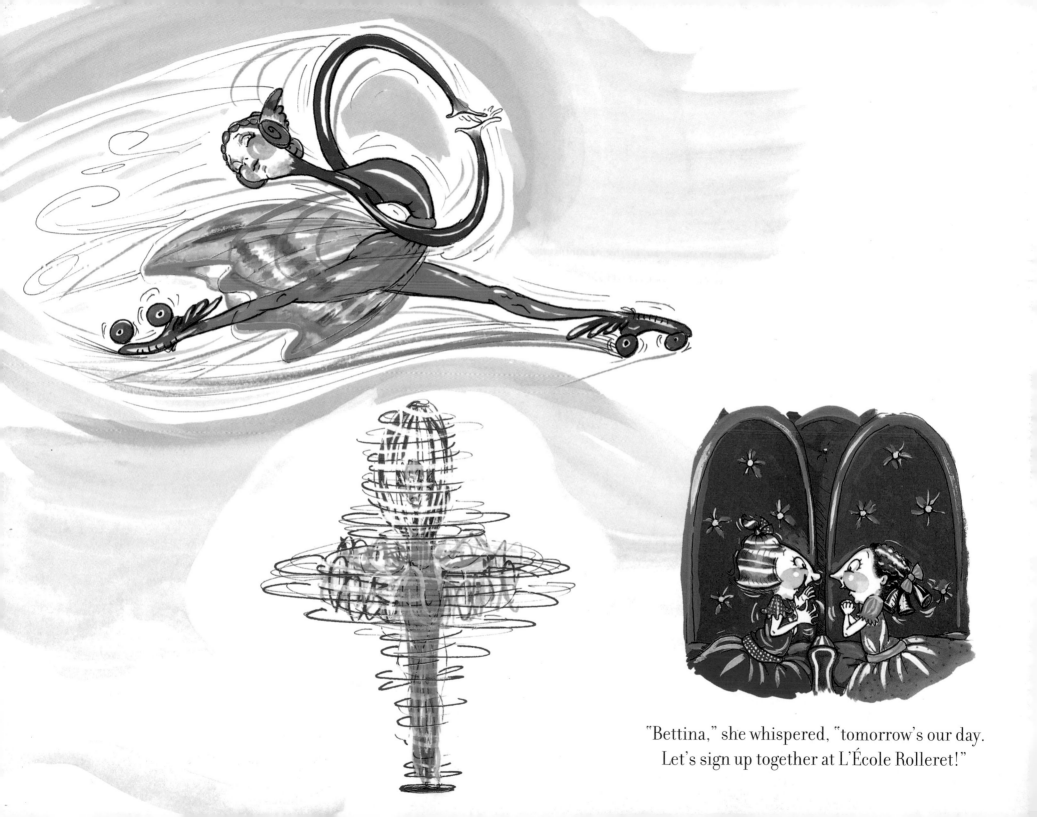

"Bettina," she whispered, "tomorrow's our day.
Let's sign up together at L'École Rolleret!"

The Rolleret School was run by Miss Flow.
    Her students were prepping for an upcoming show.
"Hard work and practice. That's what it takes.
    And don't be afraid to make some mistakes."

That night, as Priscilla lay snuggled in bed,
   Rollerina fantasies swirled in her head.
Curled up and cozy—couldn't you guess?—
   she imagined *herself* as the roller princess.

But the first day of class, things went all wrong.
    Maybe, thought Priscilla, *I just don't belong.*
The changing room was cold, with no place to sit.
    Her leotard prickled. It felt full of grit.
The skates caused a cramp, clearly too tight.
    Even her hairdo didn't seem right.

Well this stuff was nothing, petty at best.
Just to stay standing, that was the test.

Her bottom was bruised, like her elbows and knees.
"Up, up," sang Miss Flow. "Try again, please."

Priscilla gave it her all, **two hundred percent.**
She kept on those skates wherever she went.
She kept right on rolling, like she didn't have brakes.
Hard work and practice. That's what it takes.

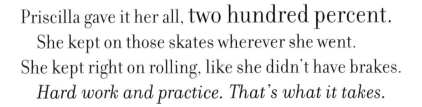

She circled and spun 'til her legs felt like lead.
Then each night she rolled herself right into bed.

Miss Flow ended class early one day.
    "I know you're all eager to work on the play.
So tomorrow, my dears, auditions will start.
    No one should worry. You'll each get a part."

That night Priscilla slept barely a wink.
Princess Rollerina, was all she could think.
If I get the lead part, I'll feel so proud.
Imagine the glitter, the roar of the crowd.

The next day at auditions, spirits were high.
Priscilla squirmed in her seat awaiting her try.

First went Bettina, with a look of alarm.

Next there was Sue, full of know-how and charm.

Then came Bianca, who went backwards the best.

And Jane was so fast you'd think her possessed.

Charlotte perfected one foot in the air.

Priscilla wiped out, but she did it with flair.

The next day, the fateful announcement was posted.
"I get to be Princess!" little Sue boasted.
"I get to wear the rhinestones and glittery gown!"
"You got the part?" Priscilla asked with a frown.

"Now Priscilla, my dear," said Miss Flow with a smile,
"you must show your skills skating freestyle.
You can really cut loose. Just do what you do.
The infinite Wind is the best part for you."

When Priscilla got home, disappointment set in.
Minute by minute her mood turned more grim.
She even skipped class the following day.
She thought she might quit the silly old play.

"What?" laughed Bettina. "What about me?
You really lucked out. I play the Tree.
And the Princess is stuck in a tower all day.
The Wind at least gets to *blow* the whole play."

Then, Priscilla had a true change of heart.
"You're right, Bettina. It is a good part.
The Wind isn't fancy, but it's flowing and free.
I'll be a great Wind. Just wait and see!"

On opening night, Priscilla felt her heart pound.
"Come along," called Miss Flow. "Gather around.
You've all practiced hard. That part is done.
All you need to do now is go out and have fun."

Tree COSTUME handle with care

Priscilla went to the stage, taking her place.
A big, beaming grin bloomed on her face.
As the curtain drew up, she rolled into the light.
She knew it right then. This was her night.

The Tree stood quite still, except for a breeze.
The Princess was bound by a magical freeze.

But the Wind was alive, it fluttered and flew.

The Wind was amazing. Oh, how it blew!

Priscilla was soaring. She felt like a star.
And if that's how you feel, then that's what you are.